JERRY PINKNEY

The Little Mermaid

LB
Little, Brown and Company
New York Boston

*F*ar out in the ocean and miles below the surface, two realms sat divided by sea mountains.

On one side of the ridge lived a powerful Sea Witch whose greedy heart cast a shadow over everything that tried to flourish. On the other side, the merfolk kingdom shimmered with light. There the Sea King and his four daughters dwelled in an elaborate coral castle.

The littlest princess, Melody, possessed a beautiful voice, but she was not content to sing in the choir of mermaids like her sisters. She had no interest in sitting still on a royal throne. Instead, Melody explored relics of sunken ships and invented stories about objects she'd gathered from the wreckage. Once, she discovered a curious figurine that looked a bit like her, but for two cloth sticks where its tail should be. Melody often wondered about the world beyond her home.

"Is it true that some ships glide atop the water instead of lying splintered beneath it?" she asked her sisters. "And that a ball of fire burns over the land?"

"You and your daydreaming and silly stories!" they huffed. "Why concern yourself with the world above? Father forbids us to go there."

The King had warned his daughters to stay close to home because the Sea Witch, who had been cast out of the kingdom, would someday seek revenge. The King had declared that an ancient sea turtle act as his youngest daughter's guardian and that she should trust this wise creature to lead her true. So when Melody saw the turtle swimming up one day to take in air, she decided to follow him.

The little mermaid trailed the turtle until at last she burst through the water's surface. "Ah!" she exclaimed. How strange it felt for half of her body to be shivering in the early-morning air while her tail remained warm below.

But a fiery ball rising in the sky offered comfort. As waves crashed around her, Melody saw whales breaching, fish flying, and turtles bobbing in the foam. Beyond, she spotted a sliver of sand on the horizon.

Moving closer, Melody saw a figure on the beach. To her astonishment, it had two sticklike legs, just like the doll she'd found!

Melody was so filled with wonder that she started to sing. As her voice carried on the wind, the figure turned and waved. *A friend*, Melody thought with joy.

Just then, Melody felt a sharp tug on her tail.
Her heart beat wildly, until she was greeted sternly
by the sea turtle. Though Melody longed to speak to
the girl on the shore, she knew she must obey her
guardian and return to her kingdom.

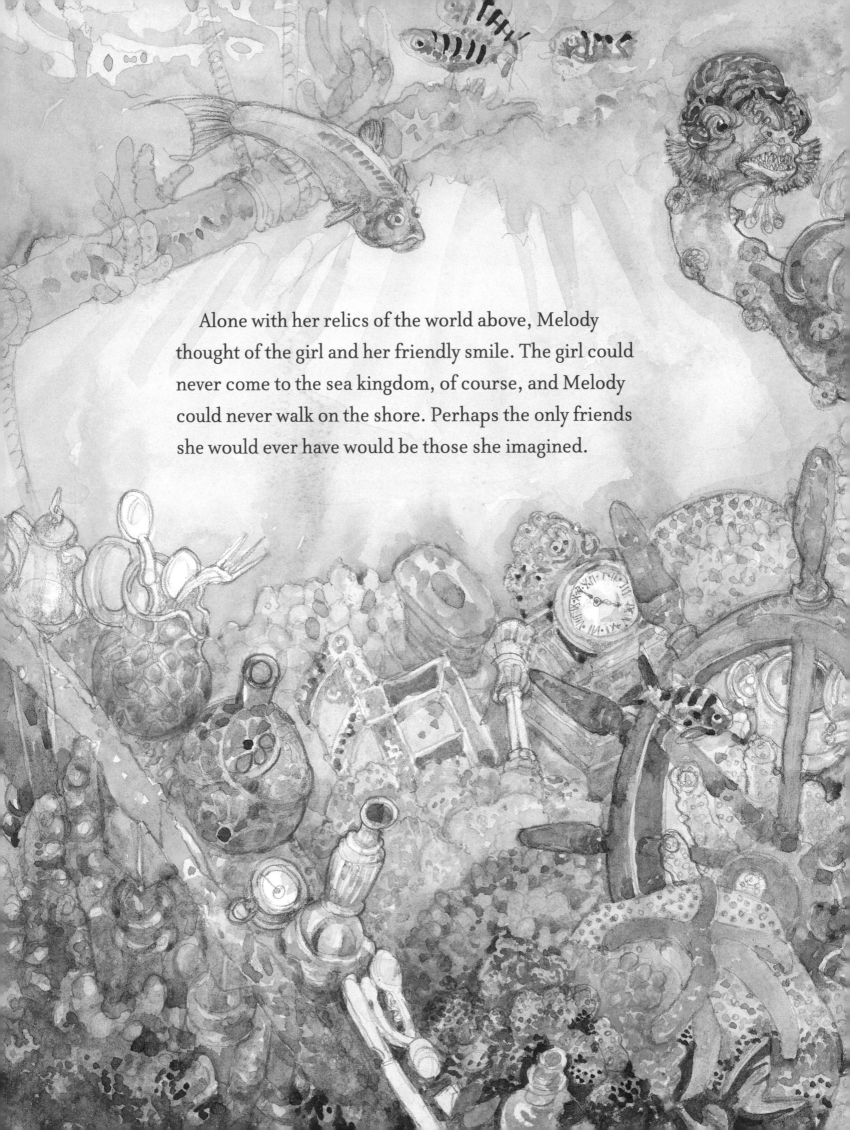

Alone with her relics of the world above, Melody
thought of the girl and her friendly smile. The girl could
never come to the sea kingdom, of course, and Melody
could never walk on the shore. Perhaps the only friends
she would ever have would be those she imagined.

"So sad, isn't it?" a voice hissed. Melody was startled to see a sea snake, slithering in the mire. "Here you are, stuck undersea...but the Sea Witch can help." Melody's eyes widened at the terrifying thought. "Do not fear," the sly creature persisted. "The Witch is not a monster, but a healer."

Melody knew the princesses were forbidden to enter the Witch's realm. It would break her father's heart to learn she'd betrayed him. And yet...who really missed her when she explored? Who listened to her stories of the spectacular world above? *No one*, she thought.

So the little mermaid followed
the snake, until suddenly, the
current caught and pulled them
toward a churning, dark void.

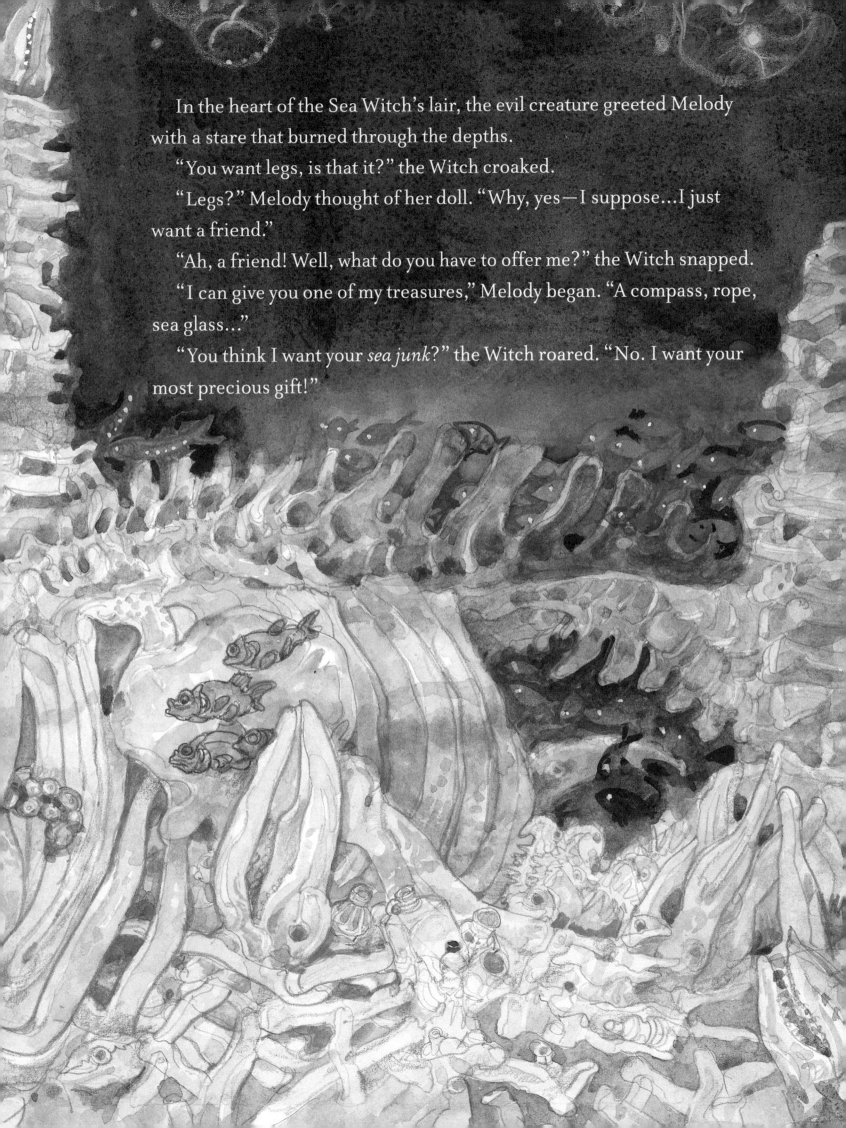

In the heart of the Sea Witch's lair, the evil creature greeted Melody
with a stare that burned through the depths.

"You want legs, is that it?" the Witch croaked.

"Legs?" Melody thought of her doll. "Why, yes—I suppose...I just
want a friend."

"Ah, a friend! Well, what do you have to offer me?" the Witch snapped.

"I can give you one of my treasures," Melody began. "A compass, rope,
sea glass..."

"You think I want your *sea junk*?" the Witch roared. "No. I want your
most precious gift!"

The Sea Witch filled a small bottle with potion. "I've heard that voice of yours...so pure, so majestic—so strong," the Witch rasped, holding out a seashell toward Melody's lips. "You can have legs, my child...but I will have your voice."

Melody shuddered. Her *voice*? She wouldn't be able to talk, or laugh, or sing!

"Come here, child," the Sea Witch beckoned. "Sing for me, and your legs, your friend, your dreams—all of it will be yours." Hesitating, Melody remembered the welcoming wave of the girl on the shore, the only one who seemed to care.

"As you wish." Melody took the shell from the Witch and began to sing her stories into it, the power of her notes rising with every breath.

When she had no melody left, she passed the shell back to the Sea Witch, who pressed the bottle into the mermaid's hand.

Once Melody had left the dark lair, she swiftly retrieved her
cherished doll and escaped to the surface out of sight of the sea turtle.
As she emerged close to shore, she saw a pearly disc hanging in the sky
that was surely one of the most beautiful things she'd ever seen. She
watched tiny turtles scurrying in the sand and birds flying overhead.
This is where I want to be, she thought.

Taking a deep breath, she drank the potion down.

As her scales fell away, Melody found it more difficult to swim as she drifted toward the shore. At last she felt fine sand against her skin and winced as a sharp shell cut into her foot. She was just starting to stand on wobbly legs when she heard a girl's voice.

"Hello!" said the smiling stranger. "It's you, isn't it? From out in the ocean?" The girl reached with a steadying hand. "I'm Zion. What's your name?"

Melody tried to answer, but no sound left her lips. Instead, she smiled back, shivering as the breeze whipped through the seaweed clinging to her body.

"Here, you can borrow this to keep warm," Zion offered, wrapping her own shawl over Melody's shoulders. "Do you want to play? I'm chasing butterflies today!"

Together the girls spent the day chasing insects and building sandcastles. Melody wanted to explore the shore's rocky caves, and Zion wanted to splash in the ocean waves. They did both, until the sun started to lower in the sky.

Though Melody could not speak, the two girls felt a surprising kinship. They both had a love of creativity and adventure. "You're the best friend I've ever had," Zion confessed, and Melody's heart sang when she heard the word *friend*.

Zion gazed intently at her now. "At first I thought you were a mermaid, but that couldn't be. Where did you come from? Why can't you speak?"

Melody retrieved the old doll that she'd brought from the sea and showed Zion. Then she picked up a stick and began to sketch a story in the sand: her fish tail, the doll, a girl waving, the Sea Witch, the seashell and the potion…

Zion gasped. "I was right—you *were* a mermaid!"

Finally, Melody illustrated the trade she had made for a human friend. Zion shook her head in disbelief. "You gave up your tail, your home, and your voice…for *me*?"

Melody nodded, and Zion threw her arms around her. "I have something for you, too."

Zion ran to her house and returned holding a glass jar with a strange object inside. "It was a caterpillar," Zion explained. "But it is growing wings, and very soon it will fly over land and sea. It's like magic! It reminds me of you."

How extraordinary, thought Melody with wonder. *An explorer. Like me.*

"But, Melody," Zion said quietly, "you should have never given up your voice…
for *anything*."

Remembering the bargain she had made, Melody spotted a seashell nearby like the one used to cast the spell. She put it wistfully to her ear, and to her surprise, a distant echo of her own voice resonated from inside. But now the sound was witchy, wild, and frightening.

Then a different sound called to her from within the shell. "The Sea Witch has risen!" came the voice of the sea turtle. "Your family is in trouble! Come!"

Oh, what have I done? Melody thought, realizing the Sea Witch had used the power of Melody's voice to grow in strength and strike in revenge.

Though Melody had no voice, she could still cry tears. She knew that to return would mean she would never walk on land again and would perhaps lose her only friend. She passed the shell to Zion, who heard the warning and the summons. "I understand you must leave," Zion said sadly. "But I'll always be your friend."

Melody drew a long breath, dove deep, and kicked furiously
as she followed the Sea Witch's screeches toward the battle. Her sisters
cried out to her. "Father's strength is useless against this dark power!"

Melody watched in horror as the Witch wrapped fat tentacles around
the King's throat. Melody felt utterly helpless, until she spotted the
seashell that had cursed her hanging around the Witch's neck. In the next
moment her guardian, the turtle, snapped the necklace free with his jaws.

Melody snatched the floating shell, and she felt the power of her own
voice rising again.

She shouted with a strength she never knew she had:

"NO!"

The Witch covered its ears as if in terrible pain. Tumbling and writhing, it drifted down, down, down…landing with one last gasp on the sharp, brittle coral the Witch had sucked the life from long ago.

The spell was broken. Melody had found her true voice—a voice that no Witch could imprison or silence.

The little mermaid could breathe again, and when she tried to kick her legs, she felt her tail flip. She opened her mouth, and such a beautiful song came out that the coral sprang back to life and the sea snakes slithered far away.

And at the shore, Zion smiled as the stormy waters became calm once again. Her friend was safe.

Now Melody's family listened eagerly as she told them about the world of people, sand, trees, and things that fly. The Sea King knew that he could not contain the adventurous spirit of his littlest mermaid.

Zion visited the shore when her treasure in the glass jar was fully transformed, and released the butterfly for Melody. It soared over the sea with its message of change and hope. And far out in the ocean and miles below the surface, the merfolk dwelled in a kingdom of light.

A NOTE FROM THE ARTIST

"The Little Mermaid" has been on my list of possible narratives to adapt for many years, but I was daunted by its extraordinary length, dark romanticism, and mature themes touching on sacrifice and spiritual immortality. Despite its challenging aspects, this beloved Hans Christian Andersen tale held on to my imagination. I came to believe that the mermaid's inquisitive nature—her overwhelming need to dare to wonder—is what draws generations of readers back to what might be considered an old-fashioned story.

When I set out to reinvent the tale in a way that might speak more directly to today's young readers, I imagined a mermaid who is a seeker, someone who doesn't just yearn for a soul mate but who also wants to experience the world. As in the original, the mermaid chooses to give up her most precious gift and the key aspect of her identity—her voice— to pursue her restless curiosity and need for companionship, accepting a potion provided by the Sea Witch. And the choice my character Melody makes to leave her friend involves a poignant sacrifice that loosely evokes the melancholy ending of the original but offers more hope; it reminds us that meaningful connection with others who are different from us, even if brief, can change our lives forever. Students of Andersen's version will notice I've made other adaptations, including shortening the timeline, changing the romance to a friendship, and dramatically cutting back the punishing nature of the original mermaid's experience. I wanted our heroine to realize the power of her voice and embrace her strength, and to bring the story full circle back to family.

Once I understood my motivation for the retelling, I created a storyboard first, focusing on the emotional and drama-tic highlights I envisioned. I then generated over 120 thumbnail sketches and more than 40 detailed concept studies, all before tackling the text. Initially, I was enticed to bring to life a world undersea, one that would honor the spectacular beauty of the ocean at a time when many of the earth's marine ecosystems are endangered. But as the project unfolded, I enjoyed exploring a reciprocal visual relationship between Melody's underwater realm and Zion's terrestrial home. While my research of the natural world was extensive, I used no live models for the mermaids. For although legend may claim they inhabit our waters to this day, I was never able to find one for reference—except in the most joyful recesses of my imagination.

For Zion, and for all who seek wonder

ABOUT THIS BOOK

The art for this book was created using pencil and watercolor on Arches cold-pressed paper. This book was edited by Andrea Spooner and designed by Saho Fujii. The production was supervised by Erika Schwartz, and the production editor was Jen Graham. This book was printed on 140gsm Gold Sun wood-free paper. The text was set in Atma Serif, and the display type was hand-lettered.